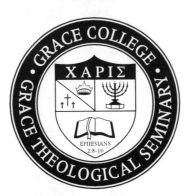

Library

Grace College and Seminary
Winona Lake, IN 46590

Kate Alone

Also by Patricia Lee Gauch

Kate Alone

by PATRICIA LEE GAUCH

G.P. Putnam's Sons New York

Library of Congress Cataloging in Publication Data
Gauch, Patricia Lee.
Kate alone.
Summary: When 14-year-old Kate's dog bites a
friend of the family she knows she must make a
decision about the dog's future.
[1. Dogs—Fiction.   2. Family life—Fiction]
I. Title.
PZ7.G2315Kat [Fic]   80-15592
ISBN 0-399-20738-4

To Christine, Chris, Sarah,
John,
and McDuff
who were there.

Kate Alone

SOMETIMES KATE THOUGHT McDUFF *was just one giant feeling. Silly. Foolish. A clown. When her mother had dragged her into that old farmhouse to see a scramble of Scottie puppies, Kate wasn't sure which was worse, the smell of diapers from all those little children, or the smell of wet papers from all the puppies. But she soon forgot that.*

Like little black caterpillars, that's what they were. Climbing over each other as if they were rocks instead of puppies. Stepping on each other's ears. Landing squat on their stomachs like collapsed chairs. Kate had to laugh.

Something of a watchdog is what we want, her mother had told Kate in the car when she had dragged her there instead of letting her watch the 4:30 movie. Something so that when Mrs. Arthur got home late from work, Kate wouldn't be so lonesome babysitting J.

Then that old gray brindle mama dog had come growling up at Mrs. Arthur. Snarling. The dog's lips pulled back around her teeth like drawn curtains.

"She's worried about your big purse." The woman laughed and tugged the mama dog away at the same time. "Any of them will make good watchdogs. They're like their mama."

Kate didn't pay attention to any of it. She hung over the side of the playpen watching for something special, something that would let her know the right dog. Then two of the larger puppies began a life-and-death wrestling match on top of the littlest puppy, who just stared patiently. Suddenly he raised his rear end like a helicopter and sat up between them, throwing them to each side. Not satisfied, he happily tackled one, then in a midair turn, pounced on the other. The three rolled around the pen in a furry circle.

"I want that one," Kate said. It wasn't easy to keep your eye and finger on the right pup when they all had tiny square whiskers on too-big heads and were constantly moving.

"The runt?" the woman asked.

"Yep, the runt." Probably not much of a watchdog, but Kate knew a clown when she saw one.

QUICKLY, KATE GRABBED the branches that hung like webs over the trail and let herself drop down onto the concrete chunks that some builder had dumped over the side of the ravine like so many stairs. At the bottom, she waited. The short steps following her were scrambling somewhere along the top of the ravine. He was still coming.

Kate picked up her skirt and took a flying leap across the river, not much more than a muddy path clogged with old gym shoes and rocks and empty Coke bottles. Then, still running, she wadded up her peasant skirt and tucked it into the legbands of her underpants.

"Kate?" a voice called down the ravine.

Kate stopped to think, thoughtfully biting her lip, then quickly she stepped across a fallen log and turned into a tiny side trail, half hidden by a battered refrigerator.

There was a ploshing of leaves behind her as feet came tumbling down the side of the ravine without the help of the concrete chunks. "Kate?"

Ahead of her lay a den of pricker bushes, dead raspberry branches hollowed against the hill. Kate glanced over her shoulder then darted in and hunched against an old shirt-covered plank that someone had imagined into a chair. And waited.

The feet hesitated along the opposite side of the stream. Then stopped. Again, they scuffled along the bank. Probably searching for a narrow place to jump. They paused. To make a leap?

Kate didn't move.

The feet crunched to a landing on the other side and started running toward her again.

"Come on, Kate!" The feet darted breathlessly. "Kate. Hey, Kate!" Then suddenly they stopped. They shuffled over to the log, quietly. Stopped. Crunched even more quietly over to the old refrigerator. Waited.

Kate could feel her breath moving in and out, but so softly her shirt didn't even move.

Now there was no sound of feet. No crunching. Kate lifted her head and moved her eyes from side to side like a deer. Suddenly, she heard the slightest crack. A twig. Feet. Not more than a yard away.

Slowly, soundlessly, she let her hands drop to the ground. When she heard the crackle again, she crouched under the makeshift door, sprang to her feet, and leapt at the sound.

"J!" she shouted and bared her teeth at him.

The eyes she met just widened as they looked up at the voice. But they didn't flinch. They wouldn't dare. If J. didn't know anything else, he knew that his fourteen-year-old sister did not like him to flinch. He just hiked his soccer ball up under his arm, waited a respectable amount of time, then started.

"Why did you run, Kate? Are you in a hurry? But if you are, why did we take the ravine-way home through Simpson's Woods? Are you not telling me something, Kate?" Nonstop.

Kate blew the strand of hair that had fallen across her eye to one side, then elbowed her way past J. Furious. That was the trouble with him. One of the troubles. His questions didn't come one at a time like normal people's. They came in threes or fours or fives, for Pete's sake.

He kept it up. "Does it have something to do with McDuff, Kate? He's my dog, too. Sort of. Is Duff coming home today?"

He really was not going to stop. Kate pulled her skirt out of the legbands and let it drop. Immediately a branch of a log snagged the hem. Ever since she had decided to give up her jeans for dresses—it had been four weeks since the first day of school—she had had trouble getting through woods with her usual ease. She lunged up the rising path anyway.

J. tried to keep up, catching the branches that flipped back at him out of Kate's way.

"Or is it those girls, Kate? Is that it? You didn't want to have to pass those girls playing soccer. Right, Kate?" He unlatched his shirt from a particularly nasty pricker bush with his free hand. "Didn't you want them to see you, Kate?"

Kate cut across sideways and climbed onto a castaway TV table that formed a convenient ledge on the ravine wall. She knew J. would have trouble with it. There were any number of brothers she could have gotten. One a year older, but good and tall, someone she could play basketball with every summer night. Someone four years older even, who could drive a car and take her to soccer games. Or out for pizza with his friends. No, she had to get stuck with this. A ten-year-old genius who had all the answers. And questions. Kate looked over her shoulder at him. Even his freckles weren't normal. They didn't sprinkle themselves like other people's. They clumped in puddles across his nose. All over his cheeks. His hands.

Kate blew out another breath and pulled herself up onto the ravine bank from the ledge.

"It's either Duffy or those girls. I just know," J. kept on. When a pricker bush pulled his soccer ball out of his arms and sent it bouncing down the ravine, he stopped temporarily, but then, retrieving it, took the ravine wall with fresh determination and came scrambling after her.

When he reached her heels, he started again, "You may want to keep it a secret, Kate, but I know." That was when he stepped on the back of her shoe and her heel popped out.

Kate stopped, and slowly turned. Then she shouted up into the trees. "THE . . . TROUBLE WITH YOU, J., IS THAT YOU . . . DON'T . . . KNOW . . . SILENCE . . . IS . . . A . . . VIRTUE!"

"It's Duffy, isn't it." He got his last word in. He always had to. Kate just glared at him.

"The soccer game?"

"What you don't know, J.," Kate began, almost in a whisper, her face narrowing toward his, "is that I didn't see any soccer game. Did you see a soccer game? Well, then, you see things, J., and are probably crazy, which doesn't surprise me. String-bean girls pushing balls around and giggling like two-year-olds at their boy coaches, giggling, J., is not a soccer game. And I didn't see one."

J. didn't say anything.

"And, J., Duffy is my dog. Nobody else's. And maybe I know he's coming home from the vet's today. Maybe Mom called me. But, J., if I want to hurry home to hang crepe paper from the ceiling and hide bones all over . . ." she flicked her fingers at a rock, toward a fallen tree, an old leather boot, "it's my business. Because Duff is my dog, and because a person needs to be ALONE!"

A squirrel darted through the tangle of river bushes at Kate's last words, but the green eyes that stared back at her didn't flinch. And when she turned around, flicked her skirt at him and started through the path, J. just marched along behind her as if he were following his general, had just gotten his orders and taken them like a man. For a minute.

". . . even so, Kate . . ." he started again.

But this time Kate shrieked as loud as she could, "HELP!" and she suddenly grabbed his soccer ball, dropped it ahead of her, and dribbled the ball through the woods.

"Wait, Kate." J. scrambled after her.

But Kate looped the ball out a break into the open field, then turning and spinning across the field, her skirt circling out around her legs, she shrieked "help" over and over. J. couldn't get near her. At one turn when he tried to snatch the ball, she made a ring around him, then gave the ball a swift kick, and whipped it across the field toward an old rusted swing set someone had left in the weeds. As it passed the broken seat chain, she finally shouted, "Score."

J. sagged down at her feet to catch his breath. "Duffy's definitely coming home today. Am I right, Kate?"

IT WAS FOUR THIRTY. The wreath on the family room wall smelled stronger than it had ten months before when Kate's father had nailed it up. Streaming from the wreath's nail to the fireplace poker to the stack of magazines on the floor to the top of the shadeless lamp was a single, twisting, red piece of crepe paper. Another climbed its way from the couch, to a Lego fort tower to a three-legged, listing worktable pushed into the corner. Under the table in clear view lay a piece of chewed gutlike rawhide. A prize.

The room was a cluttered carousel of streamers, dishes and toys, but settled comfortably in the center of it was the brown couch, out of which stuck a tangle of arms and legs mixed up in great confusion with a patched green blanket. The television picture was on in front of the couch without sound.

"I am going to tell you something you may not believe, J." Kate's voice had a far-off mythic quality she used when she was planning to tell him something properly mystical and fascinating.

"Yes, Kate." J.'s hair usually stuck out at angles away from his head, but peeping out of the green blanket it looked almost electrified.

"We are the center of the world . . . the universe." Her "center" took on a boldness J. recognized.

For once J. didn't say anything. Hard as it was. There was no sense in risking saying something wrong when Kate was obviously in a mood to talk to him. Maybe his eyes registered a certain amount of doubt, but Kate was talking to him at least. He liked that.

"How do you know?" he said cautiously. He reached down and scratched his toe. It was right next to Kate's, and he wasn't altogether certain which toe was his for a minute.

"Doesn't it feel like it, J.? Feel it right here. Warm. Feel your back against the cushions. Can't you feel all the planets spinning around you? The moon. Jupiter. All its little moons. Spinning and spinning."

J. stayed real quiet for a minute, waiting for that feeling. It did feel sort of warm. He wondered if that was the same thing.

"Yes, I feel it, Kate. Pluto and Mars." He closed his eyes, trying to get into the mood.

"And all the people in this world are moving. Spinning. They don't know that when they walk into the grocery store and pick out their Wheaties and their

Granola Bars they are moving around the Great Brown Couch."

"They don't, do they?" J. let his toe go, confident that he'd find it again if he needed to.

"And when they all get in their little Volkswagens and speed and speed down the expressway or down Liberty Corner Road, they don't know they're also spinning around the Great Brown Couch."

"Boy, are they going fast, Kate. Speeding and spinning." He hiked himself up the buttoned side to look at her. She always got that swami look when she was in one of these moods.

"Even Mrs. Holland, that miserable, crabby old lunchroom lady, who won't let anyone even whisper at lunch, is spinning around at the same time she's walking down the aisles of her stuffy lunchroom."

"Everybody's moving, Kate. Mom and Dad, too. And Susan." For some reason he imagined everybody floating in the air like Mary Poppins.

But then it all got out of hand. "But Kate," he sat up suddenly, "How can we be the center of everything? If we're the center, isn't the universe off kilter? I mean, what about the part of the world that's under us? Won't we wobble and crash into someone?" He was terribly disturbed by the thought of the hulky lump that was China and Russia and the stuff in the middle that his teacher Mr. Jephson said was a huge molten mass.

Kate sat up in the middle of the blankets. There they went again. Those questions. And sure enough three in a row. "You see, J., that is the trouble with you. You only think in squares. You don't know how to think in circles."

J. looked wounded. He had loved being in the warm center with Kate. "But, Kate, I only worried if our center was the center, our world would get out of whack, and then the rest of the universe wouldn't work so well, would it?"

But it was too late. Kate had pulled her knees into her own corner of the couch, and the front door had opened at the same time, and there was no time for J. to have another chance.

"Duffy!" Kate's feet sank into the deep cushions as she stood up on the couch and looked through the doorway, but then she slumped down. It was only her sister Susan and Susan's boyfriend, Pat.

Kate pulled the blankets over her head and dropped her shoulders down into the couch, which seemed to shrink by the moment. J.'s brows knit as he listened for the feet to come into the room.

"I don't believe it," a voice announced.

That beginning didn't surprise Kate for one minute. Out of the corner of her eye she could see her nineteen-year-old sister, her hands stuck into her waist, half-smiling and gasping as she looked around the family room.

"This has got to be the last straw. Poor mother has to come home from work to this? Cereal dishes on the table. Magazines piled in the corner. Food under the chair. It's like a ticker tape parade, right here in our house. Pat, do you believe this?" Susan's neat fluffy brown hair swung from side to side as she picked her way through the room as if if she touched anything it would give her leprosy. "This house is mad, and everyone in it is mad!"

Pat twisted his mouth to one side and clicked serious agreement. He was almost one of the family. Not too tall, but with a thick, wrestler's neck and brown devilish eyes which always had a hint of a trick in them, whenever Susan was around, he was around. "This time, you've gone too far, Kate and J.," he clicked.

Susan picked up the dishes and stacked them in her arms. "It just isn't fair to Mom," she mumbled and shook her head. She didn't notice that Pat had dropped to the floor behind the couch and was crawling on his hands and knees around the side.

J. poked his head up like a periscope, sensing danger, but he couldn't turn his neck the ninety degrees necessary to discover the enemy. Pat crawled undetected and lay down under the couch arm. Then, just as Susan walked by balancing her dishes, Pat reached up around the side, grabbed J.'s leg, and pulled him, flailing his arms and legs, and screaming.

"No. Kate, help! Help! Pat's struck again," he screamed, punching his nineteen-year-old foe with all his might.

Whenever the two of them met, it was understood that there would be a contest of battlefield proportions, which Kate usually ended up a part of. One time J. had found himself tied to the basement pole like a white captive. Just like during the French and Indian War, Pat had told him. Another time Pat had pulled him up a magnolia tree and left him there.

This time Pat had him by the leg and was pulling him upside down across the family room like a bag of potatoes. "I need to take this young 'un back to the plantation,". Pat dramatized. "He's a wicked 'un, Mother!" He shook his head and pursed his lips worriedly at Susan, who had sat down with resignation in the middle of the floor with one of the red streamers resting lightly on her ear.

Across the room, Pat dragged J. out into the hall, where J. suddenly puckered his lips, flipped himself out of Pat's grip, and ran into the dining room.

"I'll get 'im, Mother. Don't you worry none," Pat shouted. J. ran toward a forest of plants his father had put by the window to get a good day-long sun. The Chinese Aralia in the middle, the spider plants on the small tables and the impatiens flowering quietly, their pinkish blooms dusting the floor. J. took the forest by surprise. He slipped in between the spider plants, but Pat reached over and grabbed his arm before he could sink down behind the Chinese Aralia. Over went the Chinese Aralia, crashing into the spider plants which toppled like dominoes into the row of impatiens.

Susan's eyes shot up at the ceiling. "Pat! Oh, God. Oh, my God." The world had just sunk into her shoes. She glanced at the clock: 4:40. Without another word, she ran for the broom closet, but there was fear in her voice when she shouted from the laundry room: "Kate! J.! The broom. Where's the broom? Mom will be home in ten minutes!"

"Oh, yeh," J. answered from the forest. "It's in the backyard. It's the first Gatling gun in my fort." He hated to part with it, but even J. knew the situation had reached serious proportions. The first Gatling gun would have to go.

"Oh, my God," Susan mumbled and ran out the door, leaving it open to the fall flies, which still hung hopefully on the screen.

Pat took a few handfuls of dirt, put them back in the closest pot. "You shouldn't have struggled, boy. Ya know I'm going to win. The Yanks always win!" His brown eyes danced at J. threateningly. Always that mischief just at the edges of them. Kate took a piece of paper and pushed some of the dirt into piles. She had to admit, no one could be as dramatic as Susan. Almost never home now that she went to college, when she came, listening to her was like listening to someone on the six o'clock news—words, words, words.

Now Susan stood outside the screen door. "The broom is full of mud and double knotted to the gas meter! Is the vacuum cleaner anywhere?" she shouted, pressing her face against the screen to make sure everyone hadn't deserted.

"Mrs. Jackson borrowed it," Kate shouted back.

Susan turned down the stairs, hell-bent for Mrs. Jackson's.

Kate puffed out a sigh of relief, went back into the family room, climbed into the Great Brown Couch and stared at the silent TV set. Three talk-show partici- pants chattered and laughed soundlessly at each other. J. climbed in next to Kate, and Pat climbed onto the other side. They all sank into the floaty cushions.

Kate looked at J. J. looked at Pat. Pat looked at Kate, then J. "I don't know what I'm going to do with you two. You are trouble with a capital T. Trouble!" They both stared at him, then in a perfectly synchronized moment, they all burst out laughing. Not soft snickers. None of them was that sort of person. They all laughed hard, punching each other to remind each other they were enemies, then scooping up great heaves of new laughter from the latest punch. Kate looked around at the streamers which circled the couch and crossed above them like a carousel. She was glad Duffy was coming home today. It was just the right time.

FIVE THIRTEEN. Kate just sat there when they all left. She could have opened the brown package with all the stamps on it addressed to her. It was either the cosmetics she ordered from her *Contemporary Woman* magazine or the power microscope she ordered on a thirty-day trial from *Soccer World*. She could have answered the phone call from Kathy Ryan instead of telling J. to say she had had an exhausting day and was sleeping. She didn't do any of those things. She just watched the soundless TV—a pink lion versus a small bald hunter—and waited.

The Great Brown Couch was Duffy's, too. He had just the place he liked to sit. By Kate's head. He discovered he could get up on the couch when he was only a pup. That same day he discovered that if he made enough trouble, people would come running to feed him.

An uppity black rectangle with uppity pointed ears and a stomach so close to the ground that his hairs swept the kitchen floor, Duff had still been only a few weeks old when he discovered that his people ate all day long. Kate always came in and settled down with something in a box that smelled crackery, leaving the wrappers where Duff could take in the salty smell. Susan preferred popcorn, and the buttery smells lingered long after she had licked her last fingers. J. ate rolls of bologna, and his fingers smelled of it even at bedtime.

So after only three days in the house, Duffy went into action. When Kate came home from school, he circled her feet like a whirligig, spinning around and around her, then spinning into circles of his own. Kate couldn't believe he was putting on that big show for her. She sat down in the middle of the floor and let him run up on her lap and lick her face. But when she got up to leave, he stood like a little sergeant at the door, his squat legs firm, and his tail straight up like a pointed flag. His brown eyes, the white just showing like moon crescents, stared at her. Obviously, she was guilty of something.

"But what do you want, Duff?"

He stared.

"Come on, Duff. What?"

He just resettled his legs in a solid stance.

"If you can't tell me, I'm going." But when Kate had started to push past him, he had run back in another circle, got a good healthy start, then ran smack into her legs with his front paws.

"Duffy!"

He ran back, made the same quick circle and charged again, this time lingering to stare up at her with mournful, begging eyes.

When Kate still puzzled over this attack, he turned his tail in reverse and without a pause ran over to his bowl and, picking it up with his front teeth, threw it. It rolled across the kitchen floor and crashed into the kitchen chairs.

"Oh, that's it, is it?" Kate said. "All right, Pushy. You can have a snack, too." And she filled his bowl with milkbones and returned to the family room couch. Duff gulped down the milkbones, then with his new energy, he charged back into the family room and took a helicopter leap onto the couch, cozying himself neatly by Kate's hair. It looked as if she were wearing a black bonnet.

"You really are a clown."

He even got in trouble like one. The worst was when he started spraying anything over a foot tall that anyone set down. Mother's shopping bags. Dad's briefcase. J.'s bat. Anything that looked like a tree. Even Kate knew her mother was right about trying the operation. Duff was old for that kind of operation—most dogs were "fixed" when they were pups, not when they were three years old; but sometimes it helped. If anyone could take an operation, or anything else, it was feisty little Duff. Kate wasn't worried about that.

Clown. She reached up by her hair out of habit. The spot was empty, but the next time the door creaked open and her mother called out, "Kate," Kate knew McDuff was finally home.

ONE TIME KATE HAD FIGURED the kitchen cupboards had thirteen layers of different colored paint on them. Lilac and chartreuse among them. There were so many layers that all the edges were rounded. You could hit your head on a corner when you were trying to reach for the Wonder Woman glass and it wouldn't even hurt. The whole kitchen was like that. Rounded. A pile of clothes, mostly towels, on the washer and drier. A pile of dried but not-put-away dishes, mostly bowls, on the sink. A pot simmered on every burner of the stove with lids piled where they would fit.

Just now people even seemed piled around the table. But they weren't quiet mounds like the clothes or dishes. Everyone was talking and moving at the same time. A noisy blur. Except for J. who stirred something on the stove, alternately sprinkling in cinnamon and tarragon vinegar.

Kate's father was carefully smelling the bread and

murmuring, "Mmmmmmmmm." He shook his head approvingly. Tall and thin with glasses that made his eyes seem all the more dreamy, he was an accountant with a city bank, but he didn't seem like one. He grew plants, listened to FM, and had love affairs with things like homemade bread and gazpacho soup and waffles with pecans.

"What I was saying to Dad is that I think something has to be done about this house," Susan said. "It is bad enough that the outside looks like the house that Jack built . . ."

"Mmmmmmmmm," Kate's father had just discovered the crust. "There's honey on this crust." His brow wrinkled with delight.

J.'s nose twisted. "I need more cinnamon or more potatoes. This can't be what the Confederates ate at Sharpsburg."

"Probably you need more salt," Mrs. Arthur said. She walked over to the stove, dipped her finger into the pot, tasted it, and shuddered.

"I mean the potting shed across the front door is no easy thing to explain, even if people have seen your plants, Dad, but I had to bring Pat into a family room that looked like the . . ."

". . . the Cub Scout paper collection center," her father helped her. "I remember a bread made of oatmeal and bananas and walnuts. Mmmmmmmmm."

He picked out a nut, smelled it approvingly, then let it slip into his mouth.

J. took another potato and started to peel it over the middle part of the stove. "Mom, do you think the Yanks ate the same kind of soup as the Rebs? How could either of them stop to make a fire when they were in the middle of a battle?" He clipped off a particularly troublesome peel and threw it into the pot. "And what if they didn't have bowls?"

Kate didn't hear a thing. Not even the questions. All she could hear was Duffy's soft munching on a leathery treat that he had discovered under the toaster-oven stand. She picked up the tablecloth and looked at him. He really was home. He lay between her feet, his legs spread out like a starched shirt drying on a clothesline. He shook his head and grumbled at the sinewy piece, but when he caught Kate's eye, he stopped and looked at her, those mischievous rims, his feet tensed, ready for a quick getaway.

"Silly dog." She nudged his side with her foot and he went on comfortably munching.

"I couldn't find either the broom or the vacuum cleaner." Susan was still talking.

Kate's mother, a stocky woman, with thick features and brownish curled hair pushed naturally back of her ears, nodded. No makeup, a slight blush to her cheeks from bicycling ten miles to work every day. Even thick arms. She moved slowly, as if buried down in the middle of her there was a kind of understanding of all this confusion.

"The vacuum cleaner's at Mrs. Jackson's." She sliced the roast and put another slice on Mr. Arthur's plate.

"Mmmmmmmmmm," he replied.

"I know. But Mrs. Jackson wasn't home. I finally used Dad's car broom, but . . ." Susan pushed back in her chair.

"J.," her mother interrupted, "you're going to have to get a bigger pot, if you're going to make that much soup. How many troops are you planning on anyway?"

J. dropped the last potato into the pot and the water splashed over the sides and steamed on the stove.

"A bigger pot, J.," his father said without looking up.

"It's Kate, that's the real problem." Sue looked across at her sister.

Kate bent down and grabbed the treat from Duff, then threw it in back of her. Duffy hiked his rear up until the treat landed, then, his legs spinning like propellers, dashed across the kitchen.

Mrs. Arthur stepped over to refill a serving dish with creamed corn. "That operation didn't hurt old Duff any. He's as feisty as ever."

"Kate's fourteen. She should be out of the house

more, Mom. Sometime anyway. But what does she do? She sits on that couch, watches a TV set that isn't even on, and reads advertisements in magazines." Susan looked at her father as if this piece of news would stun him.

"Tonight on Channel 13 the Boston Symphony is playing the overture to *Tannhäuser.*" He started to hum it.

Susan sat down and blew a breath up through the hair that fell across her forehead. Kate slipped down under the table and took Duff's head in both hands. His scruffy wirelike hair smelled of veterinarian. She wasn't sure where the operation had been, but it wasn't at this end. And it made her feel comfortable to know he was the same feisty old Duffy. She pushed his head down, and scrambling between chairs jumped and ran to the stove.

"Save me, J., Save me!" She cowered behind J. whose forehead puckered from smelling his Confederate soup.

"Don't you see, Dad. That's what I mean. The TV set, the couch, the dog. That is her life."

"I'll save you, Kate!" J. threw his arms up like a crossing guard while Kate cowered behind them. Duffy circled the butcher block and running the length of the room pounced on J. with his two front feet. Then he started to bark.

Mrs. Arthur laughed. The skin on her high cheek-bones crinkled at the edges. Mr. Arthur took the crust carefully, cut it in half and dipped one piece into the last pool of sauce on his plate.

"But, Mom, she has chances. Kathy Ryan is still a nice girl, boy crazy, but nice. She and some other girls play soccer every afternoon back by the ravine. The only place Kate plays soccer is in the living room."

"It's a big room, dear," Mrs. Arthur said, still smiling at the fracas at the other end of the room. "Come on, Duffy, don't stand for that."

Kate teased the piece of hide around J.'s knees, then pulled back. Duff jumped on him again. "Hey! I'm not a bad guy, Duff." Duff took another kitchen-wide run and came winging at J.

"You know he won't stand for anyone hurting Kate . . . or any other Arthur," Kate's mother laughed.

Kate grabbed Duff's ear as he came near her, turned him around and started to run into the pantry, when suddenly a hissing exploded on the stove. The Confederate soup had sprung up in churning boils.

"Turn off the heat, J., and get a larger pan." No one moved. The soup flowed over the sides. Susan sat down. Mr. Arthur looked startled, and Mrs. Arthur ran across the room toward the pan cupboard.

"Help!" J. shouted. "It's running all over. It's getting wrecked."

Kate stood in the corner, grasping the piece of hide, and laughed as J. hopped around the stove waving his arms. Mrs. Arthur scrambled through the stacks of pans looking for the largest one.

"This is like the Spaghetti Pot," Kate said over the clanging pans. "Watch out, J., because the potatoes will grow. Up, out of the pot."

"I can't find that pan!" Mrs. Arthur mumbled. The soup still spluttered. "Turn off that heat, J."

"Out of the magic pot the potatoes will grow across the stove." Duffy was leaping against Kate's knees. "Across the kitchen. Across the family room. Even up the stairs."

J. turned off the heat but the stove still steamed. Kate knew he was listening to her potato story from the way he hunched his shoulders. She had hooked him again.

"Ah, I'll just have to use this big thing." Mrs. Arthur grabbed a turkey broiling pan and started across the room.

"Potatoes up the chimney!" Kate shouted.

But suddenly, Duffy started to growl. Kate looked down. Duff wasn't playing. The mischievous moons were gone. His ears were back and his nose lowered as he stared at Mrs. Arthur and the broiling pan. She walked slowly, but Mr. Arthur put his fork down.

"Mae," he said very quietly, "don't move."

The kitchen grew absolutely still. Just the last boiling in the pot. J. still leaned against the stove. Kate stood in the corner. Susan, horrified, kept her eyes on her mother.

Duffy's lip curled in an S over two sharp white teeth.

"Now . . . Kate. Speak to Duffy quietly," Mr. Arthur said easily, naturally. "Then throw the piece of gut back toward the family room door."

Kate felt the rough gut rubbing against her hand. "Come on, Baby." Her voice felt shaky. "Duff. Duff. Here's a treat." Then she gave the gut a hefty toss toward the open doorway.

Duff looked at the door, looked back at the angry, big glittering pan, then with a blink, he charged across the kitchen after the hide treat, his tail wagging like a propeller.

"KATE, CAN I COME?" "Kate, can't I come?"
"Come on, Kate, let me come." Kate pulled on her
sweat shirt marked Harvard and started out the door.
She didn't even bother saying no. Duffy scrambled out
ahead of her, as far as he could go on the leash. Extra
long, but not long enough for Duff.

At the gate, Kate slipped through the gateway
without attempting to open it past the uncut grass. She
was skinny enough, but she couldn't bother with
things like knobs and gate handles or anything else.
Not right now. Kate was mad. All right, angry.
Everyone had jumped on Duff. All of them.

The dry leaves, restless from a new fall wind,
gossiped around her. Some of them fell around her
shoulders as she reached the sidewalk and started
scuffling down the hill. Duffy pulled against the leash.
They'd probably have something to say about that, too.
Well, she'd have an answer. Ten weeks in dog obedience class hadn't done all that much for Duff, even

though he had received runner-up "best behaved," but that was because Kate couldn't be bothered stopping every five seconds to say "Heel!" or "Stay!" or any of those nice chanty things the dog obedience leader had taught her. But she and Duff could play that game whenever they wanted.

Kate suddenly stopped.

"Sit, Duff," she commanded. Duff looked at her for a minute, then he lowered his bottom like a stone sinking in water. His moon eyes searched hers, afraid Kate was angry with him. "Walk," Kate said sternly. Duff started off.

See, Duffy minded well if she wanted him to. She wasn't angry with Duff anyway, for Pete's sake. Some things made Duff grumpy. Dad's glass-cutting tools sent him into circles of barking. When J. cut the lawn, Duff always tried to attack the lawn mower. He didn't like metally looking things. He was just guarding his people, and he only nipped at a something. He didn't bite. Probably that vet, or someone there, had stirred him up. Rattled his cage or something. It wouldn't happen again. After all, McDuff had only been home a few hours.

Duffy strained at the leash as a gray squirrel darted noisily across the fallen leaves. Then, when that seemed hopeless, he pulled the other way in time to check a passing bicycle. Nothing escaped old Duffy.

Smart, that's what he was. They needn't all have gotten so excited. Duff was smart as a whip.

Kate smiled as Duff pulled her along down the descending walk. Why, she never would have seen that badger hole last spring if Duff hadn't pulled her directly to it. Funniest hole. Big, not small. A hole Hobbits should live in, sort of peopley with an entrance and exit. When she had looked it up later, she had learned badgers even have their own bathrooms. Then she realized that Duffy had known that, too.

Duffy sniffed the leavings of the St. Bernard who always walked the same path they did. Disappointed or surprised at the magnitude, he strutted on. Stuffy little Scotsman. Kate crossed the street to avoid walking in front of a brown two-story bungalow. The mail box said: RYAN. I hate that girl, Kate said to herself. All right, dislike. Kathy Ryan was a real 100 percent sometime friend. The one thing Kate couldn't forgive was a sometime friend. Sometimes ready to go to the movies with you. Sometimes ready to study with you. Sometimes willing to put on sneakers and play soccer with you. All unless something—someone—better came along to ask you to go to the high school football game on Saturday afternoon. Boys had wrecked Kathy Ryan. Paul Lorn, in particular. Who needed a friend like Kathy Ryan, for Pete's sake. Not Kate Arthur. She reached down and scruffed Duff's neck.

Duffy you could count on. She could just hear a lot of people saying that was a stupid thing to say, but no one was listening. No judge or jury. Duffy would curl up next to her when she did her algebra. Her biggest problem with Duff was keeping his big dumb clown head off her book. And he was the only dog she had ever known who could play soccer.

A gray cat dashed across the street into the bushes by the corner house, carrying a mouse. Duff grew frantic and pulled so hard at the leash his front paws were in the air. When the woman who lived on the corner came out to save the cat, Duff started barking. His don't-push-me-around bark.

Hurriedly, Kate pulled him across the field which turned into Tower Hill. The next hill to Simpson's field, it seemed to look across the lower hill and it was a nest of intriguing smells for McDuff. Below her the street lights had just turned on, though it was still twilight, and ahead the blinking red light on the top of the water tower had begun its blinking. The tower didn't look so bad at this time of day. No ugly, scaling green paint. Kate climbed through the pricker bushes, the thorns snagging the leash and pulling at her dress. Dresses were for the birds. Even if a person did look beautiful in them.

At the top Kate undid the leash and let Duff run. "Go on, you old Scotsman." Duff didn't wait for the order. He dashed like a wound-up mechanical car just turned loose on a carpet. Nose first, he tunneled under the matted undergrowth, then he pulled back and whipped around to nose out a new tunnel, snorting with exhilaration in between. Time and time again, his short stubby legs propelled him across the field to another patch of ground. Just like a mechanical toy car, turning, spinning around.

Kate sat down outside the fence that protected the water tower and stuck a weed in her mouth. Fall hadn't left much sweetness in it. Evening shadows from the few pine trees began to stretch across the dried fields. The lights from the streets below brightened now, stringing out like old-fashioned lanterns. Still, it was only twilight, a gray time.

"Hey, Duff, save some field for tomorrow," Kate shouted. She lay back in the high grass and crossed her legs up in the air. She could see her foot against the sky, bigger than a hundred stars. She liked places like this where she could see the edges of things, the roads below like lines on a giant map. The tower above her. She tried to imagine all of the universe, the thousands of milky stars and moons whirling around this tower. This big green mushroom. At least this time J. wasn't pushing his way into her head. Big freckleface question mark. Quiet was what he had to learn.

The black mechanical car finally ran down and

snuffled along the fence until he came to the gate where he discovered a gaping hole had been dug. A hole big enough for a dog, a person, for that matter. Duff sniffed under the gate as far as he could risk.

"Hey," Kate yelled. "You want to meet that mushroom, Duff? Or do you just want to be alone?" Duff ducked back out quickly, rear end first, stopped for a minute to stare down the gate, which rattled menacingly in the wind, then dashed over to Kate.

"Clown." She smiled. She had forgotten she was mad at anyone.

MR. ARTHUR LIFTED the plant's delicate lacy leaf, then let it drop. He dipped his finger into the soil, rubbed it very slowly between his fingers, then, lowering his glasses, looked at each grain carefully. Finally, he closed his eyes with disgust and smelled it.

"Mae!" he called upstairs. "This soil is sour. The Ph level has *dropped*. It is absolutely atrocious! The leaves are screaming. Look at them. They're screaming! Mae!" He shook his head, the weight of his obvious sorrow slowing each sideways turn.

He nearly missed seeing the soccer ball shoot in a straight line from the kitchen to the hall and ricochet off the front door, directly into the living room.

"Fantastic, Pat!" J. shouted, as he ran after the ball.

"Don't hit my mirror," Kate said. She had finally opened the package with the stamps, and it was, indeed, the exotic cosmetic kit complete with Chimera oriental blue and brown lip rouges and powders from the East. Kate, sitting cross-legged, a family trait, puckered at the floor-length mirror, while Duffy gnawed a soup bone contentedly by her knee. Blue just wasn't her color, not on the lips anyway. She dabbed some over the brown on her eyelids and opened and shut her eyelids.

"I have beautiful green eyes," she said to herself. "J., come look at my eyes. Anyone has blue eyes. Anyone. But my eyes are really green. Greener than yours, J. Cat green. Cleooooopatra green," her voice trailed off as she widened her eyes to circles, and then sneered them into a half-opened sexy look. She certainly could have any boy if she wanted one. "J!" she shouted.

"Pat, no, don't. Don't!" She heard J. scream and laugh at the same time. "No, Pat, I really mean it. Please don't." No one could beg like J. when he got into a bind with Pat. "Please, Pat," he wailed. Kate crawled around the corner and looked into the long narrow living room. Crowded with stacks of books piled all over the floor between leftover furniture that her mother called antique, it looked more like the storeroom of the local library.

"J.," she said once more.

The soccer ball winged directly at her, just past her mother's nonworking French clock. She grabbed her makeup in one hand, pitched it into a corner, grabbed the ball with the other, dropped the ball between her feet, and dribbled into the living room. Pat and J. were wrestling under the piano, but quickly lunged to their feet toward her. She dribbled deftly around three stacks of books to the two gray chairs, but dodged between them just as Pat came around the other side.

At the coffee table she gave the ball a kick, then ran to the other side to catch it. J. got there first. She hipped him, then scooped the ball away with her foot. Pat stretched his foot around hers and hooked the ball away, swaying his hips from side to side toward the piano.

But that was Duffy's cue. He had been lying nose down behind the sofa. Now he darted across the floor to steal the ball from Pat. Nosing it away from him, he batted it back under the table.

"Hey! Crazy dogs off the field!" Pat shouted.

But Duff batted the ball with the tip of his nose out from under the table and between the chairs.

"Ferocious forward. *Defense. Defense,*" Pat called out and ran to the front of the room. Kate laughed, and as J. and Pat tried to head Duff off, she scooped her toe between Duff and the ball and tossed the ball in a right scoop into the hallway.

"Score!" she shouted.

Pat picked up the ball and held it up. "The fantastic furry forward and the mini-but-mighty Kate Arthur score again!" Unable to wind down, Duff careened into the dining room while the three of them trailed into the family room and sank into the couch.

Pat punched Kate as she claimed the pillow. "You're all right, Katie. Keep your hands off the ball. And your mutt off the field, but," he clicked his tongue, "you move well."

Kate twisted her mouth at him. Pat was never, but never, serious. Anyone knew that. She wasn't going to fall for any words.

She looked just the slightest bit sinister with her brown and blue eye shadow. J. always told her she looked beautiful with makeup on, like a princess from a mysterious country.

"Do you believe me, Kate?" Pat said again.

Kate couldn't believe him. On the other hand . . .

"Pat!" Susan called from the top of the stairs.

Kate toed her sock into Duffy's side and scratched his stomach. "*May*be," she said. It occurred to her at that split second, just sitting there, that Pat McIntyre was the nicest person she knew—Arthur or non-Arthur. Even if he was kidding. How many nineteen-year-old people would sit with a fourteen-year-old and a ten-year-old and say things like that. Really incredible things.

It reminded her of last year when Susan had dragged her to a high school soccer game because all of her friends had gone college-looking. Pat had gotten himself into a four-player squeeze on the ten-yard line, when he did a sort of bounce on the ball which freed it. Then he followed up with a low, lateral sweep, scooping the ball and dribbling it past seven players, as if he were in a magic tunnel. Count them, seven! If you had to have something to do with boys, that was the kind you had something to do with. Not just a boy. A person. A soccer player. A crazy. Getting to know Pat McIntyre was the one smart thing Susan had ever done, besides the time she gave Kate her outgrown green cashmere sweater.

"Pat, I'm serious. That party is already two hours gone." Susan stood at the doorway, pressed jeans, a soft blue sweater that made her blue eyes seem melty, her brown hair wisping in soft curls around her face. She didn't even have any Chimera oriental blue on her eyelids and she looked like that, for Pete's sake.

Pat roughed Duffy's head and tipped Kate's nose with his finger. "You two are tough." He grinned at J. "Sorry, J., you three. See you later."

Kate sank into the couch. All of her energy sighed out of her. "Kate, would you rather have a Rolls-Royce, a limousine, or a BMW?" Kate pulled Duffy up onto her lap, a dead-weight sack, and he rolled his moons up at her helplessly. Probably the energy in this spot, right now, was beyond the absolute energy of a star, a meteor, a hydrogen bomb.

"I think we all need to talk to these plants," Mr. Arthur mumbled in the hall. "Instead of walking through the kitchen or walking through the family room, we need to take a detour past the plants and speak to them. Whisper. Gently. Do you hear me, Kate? Mae? Do you hear me? J.? Where is everybody anyway?"

KATE NEVER LIKED THE DARK. That was why she always let McDuff sleep with her, even though his coarse black hairs got all over her pillow and sheets. That was why she always slept with socks and her pink silk underpants on—in case she had to get up and run into the front yard or something. That was why she always left the door open a crack.

So, the hall light flicking on woke her first. Not the voices. But she heard them quickly enough, too. At first she just listened: it was Susan whispering into Mom and Dad's room. Whispering. Kate drifted back into her dream for a minute. There was a water tower in her dream and weeds that climbed halfway up its legs. But the whispering bothered her. There were crying whispers. Then her mother's voice, repeating over and over and over, louder and louder, as she came through her bedroom doorway. "Oh, no. Oh, no. No."

Kate could hear the slippers scuffling quickly down the bare hall with Susan's boots running behind.

Wasn't Susan scared? Someone had broken in. That must be it. Kate reached behind her pillow to touch Duff, but he wasn't there. Then she felt along the top of the bed closer to the headboard. But the sheets were cold. She hiked herself up on her elbows and looked down the bed. Duff wasn't there either. He must have already scooted out the crack to see what was going on. Something *was* going on. Cautiously, Kate touched the floor, cold to her toes now (her heart seemed to be beating in her throat), and slowly crept to the door and looked down the hall. Her parents' door was still open. Kate listened from the upstairs step. The voices were jumbled in the front hall.

"But I don't know . . . just . . . talking."

"Surely, Susan . . . the . . . did . . . reason."

"No . . . tell you . . . not that way."

"Susan . . . there . . . couch . . . must . . ."

Kate could hear Susan's scared, crying voice. Her mother's voice was low and explaining. Kate was afraid of hearing it. She usually couldn't agree with Susan on much, but she didn't want Susan to be scared. That was when she heard Pat's voice echoing from the front bathroom.

"Oh, my God. My God." It was muffled somehow.

Kate flew down the stairs. Instinctively, she screamed at the same time. "Duffy!"

At the bottom of the stairs Susan and her mother

were staring into the hall bathroom. Pat stood staring at the mirror. Blood ran in watered rivulets down the blue sink. It was spattered all over the mirror. And smeared across Pat's mouth and cheeks.

Kate's mother held onto Pat's shoulder with one hand.

"God, I am ugly!" Pat said, opening his eyes wider at the mirror.

Kate recognized Pat's teasing voice, but there was a bitter undercut to it now, as he leaned on the sink and drew himself closer to the mirror. He couldn't seem to stop looking.

For a moment, Kate just stared, then she cried out again, "Duff!" She didn't know why.

But Susan spun around. "Duff? Duff? Keep him out of here. Do you hear, Kate? Just keep him out of here!" Her face, usually prettily long, was drained white and drawn as she spoke to Kate. Not screaming, threatening.

Kate turned around and pushed the doors open into the kitchen. "Duff!" she called. "Duff?" She crawled on her hands and knees around the table, but there was no black shadow, and she ran into the family room. "Duff?" She looked behind the Lego wall and had grabbed the couch arm when she felt something wet on her hand. It was blood, blood spattered on the Great Brown Couch. She pushed away from it and, wiping her hand on her nightgown, backed into the kitchen again, then turned.

"Duff!" The back room was black. Just shadows of books and boards stacked against the wall and piles of empty pots. But there, under the workbench, she caught a glimpse of a black, furry shadow crouched in the corner.

She flicked on the lights. The shadow cowered back against the wall, moon eyes staring guiltily up, as if it were waiting for someone to hit it.

"Duff!" Kate called a last time, but he wouldn't come to her. He crouched there, silent, scared, cowering against the brick wall.

The voices suddenly burst into the room behind her. Then a dialing ripple and her mother's voice calmly saying, "Yes, I want to bring a boy right in. A dog bite. On the mouth. Would you please contact a plastic surgeon. Parents? Yes. . . . Please, someone good with young people . . . ah . . . yes. Twenty minutes."

Kate felt her shoulders sag, her knees felt cold on the back room floor. Nothing thoughts exploded in her head. How this room was over the garage. How she should have closed the garage door. How no one had picked up the rake. Everyone always forgot.

"Oh, Duffy, why?" she suddenly begged, and she started to shake. "What are we going to do?"

For WHAT SEEMED countless door slammings and scuffling for coats, and questions and answers of the easiest and hardest kinds, like where should Pat sit, and whose car should I go in, and don't wake up J., Dad will take care of him—through all that Kate sat huddled, shaking under the workbench with Duffy in her arms. His head tucked under her chin. The wall, cold against her back. Her heart beating somewhere next to her eyes.

When the last door slammed, she waited for another, still shaking. But no next door slammed, and slowly she crawled out, pushing aside several cans of paint stacked at the side. She didn't stop to put on any lights. Not even the lights in the kitchen. She stumbled through the darkness, shoved aside a kitchen chair someone had pulled into the middle of the room to replace a light. Kicked aside Duffy's sock. In the hall, she pulled open the closet and grabbed a maroon jacket, threw it over her shoulders and pulled on J.'s boots.

No one had to tell her what people did to dogs who bite. Once she and Kathy had talked about that when the newspaper boy's dog bit a customer. The dog had been quarantined for ten days until it was certain it didn't have rabies. Then the boy's parents had had the dog put to sleep. Horrible way to put it. As if dying were like sleeping. She clipped Duff's leash on and pulled him out the front door.

The houses that terraced down the block guarded by their feathered and stiff tree shadows looked like crouching giants. Kate glanced at them suspiciously, but her head was still pounding, and she couldn't stop to be afraid. Even so, as she ran, she felt herself shaking again and tears tried to come, stung at her eyes, but she wouldn't let them, even though the street lights blurred and J.'s boots, already too big for her, slapped her legs.

At the end of the street, she could see the bricks that marked the path up the tower hill, and she found herself running that way, her feet catching in the rutted rain gulleys, her ankles twisting into them. Duffy's little feet whipped under him as he tried to catch whatever it was they were chasing. At a stone well, Kate jumped the concrete chunks and climbed. The weeds snagged the overlarge jacket which she realized wasn't hers, and her boots caught on rocks, but she kept running, allowing no time for her shaking, none for the icy air that burned the bottom of her lungs.

For some reason she went right to the water tower, took off the puffy jacket, wadded it up into a ball, and threw it over the fence. Then she felt her way to the gap under the gate and, holding on to one end of the leash, crawled under. A stone scratched her cheek, and dirt smeared into her mouth, but by twisting she pulled herself up on the other side. Then she pulled the leash.

But Duffy pulled back. The fence at night cast cell shadows against the silvered weeds. Duffy started to growl at one particularly menacing shadow that fell like a giant hand across the ground.

"Stupid dog," Kate chided. "It's nothing. It's the fence and a torn box."

Duffy pulled away from Kate, still growling, his lip curled in that S.

He wouldn't come. Kate suddenly felt terribly, terribly tired sitting on one side of the fence, Duff growling on the other. Then she lifted her eyes. Wait. She reached into her pocket and pretended to take out something which she folded into her hand, palm down.

"Treat, Duff," she coaxed. Duff's ears stood flag straight. "Come on, Duff. Treat." She put her hand under the fence slowly, with her palm closed. Duff started to sniff, then backed off suddenly as a new shadow rippled on Kate's hand.

"Oh, Duff. What happened to you? Please, Duff."

Duff pulled back. Kate bent forward again slowly but her voice changed. "Come, Duff," she said in her dog-obedience voice. "Come," she said sternly. She tried not to change her tone. Lord, she tried. Then slowly, she held out her palm-closed hand and with the other very gently pulled his leash. "Come, Duff," she said.

His eyes rolled up at the fence as the box shadow trembled with the wind, but he came forward. An inch. Another. Another. Slowly, he came, and finally his tail was through. On Kate's side.

The tears tried to come again, how they tried, but Kate shook them away. Then all at once the look in her eyes changed.

"Sit, Duff," she said. "Sit!"

The black shadow turned his ear toward her, as if deciding, then slowly lowered his bottom. Kate dropped the leash, then backed up, step by step, farther under the water tower, stepping across the tower shadows which the moon had stretched into giant legs climbing the hill. Duffy leaned forward as if to follow her.

"Sit!" Kate commanded. No nonsense now. Kate's eyes glared at him. He watched her.

Kate backed up farther until she was forty feet or

more away. "Stay!" she commanded again. Her voice echoed across the ground under the giant belly of the tower.

Then she just stood there, facing the black dot across from her. There were crickets, the sound of a car racing down Five Mile Road, hollow sounds of a night wind in dry weeds. Still the dot stayed.

Finally, Kate dropped her arms. "Come, Duff. Come." The dot wasn't sure. "Come!" she commanded, and recognizing it, Duff ran toward her, his leash trailing behind him through the weeds.

Kate looked down at him sitting between her feet, waiting for the next command, but Kate sat down, and taking him into her lap, crouched against one of the legs of the giant mushroom. When a wind gusted around her legs, she unbuttoned her jacket and pulled it over Duff's back, folding him inside. A night mist had settled over the metal legs that burrowed cold into her back. Glad for the extra big jacket, she sat there, finally letting the tears come, letting them run warm and wet down her cheeks.

"See, Duff, see you can mind. You're the same Duff. You still get the prize."

The thing she was trying not to think about was Pat.

"Pssssst!"

Kate looked up from the collar of the oversized jacket. Duff moved, ready to jump, suspicious of the new noise. Kate hadn't dozed, yet she wasn't exactly certain for a moment where she was either. Her throat felt scratchy from the minty, wet night. There were the legs, though. The giant mushroom.

"Kate!"

Then it was something. Kate turned around, holding tightly to Duff. A few feet down from the hole stood J. in his plaid bathrobe and his Eskimo slippers. There was no place he couldn't find her.

"Go home, J.," Kate told him bitterly. "Leave us alone."

J. didn't move. "I almost didn't see you in there, Kate." He shivered. "Come on, Kate. Mom's coming home from the hospital in a half hour . . . she called. Dad thought we were both asleep and went back to bed."

Kate turned her back. "You're going to catch pneumonia, J., and it's dumb coming here in the middle of the night." It occurred to Kate that one of them looked as if he were in a cage. She wasn't sure who. But if J. was going to catch cold in the middle of the night, let him.

"Kate?"

Such a big chicken sometimes. Kate could tell he was afraid she was going to yell at him or something. Way beyond the trees that lined the rear of the houses, a grayness was oozing up out of the ground. No warmth in it yet. No reds or oranges. But Kate knew it was the sun. Day would be coming soon. And she felt tired inside. That was it. Tired from the inside out. She clutched Duffy tighter.

"Kate?" J. still gripped the metal fence, his smallish face looking through one of the diamond-shaped holes. She saw him suck in a breath and saw his mouth weaken at the edges. "You have to come home, Kate. You can't stay out here. It's cold in there." He stopped to catch his breath and keep it all together. "Please, Kate, come home."

What was at home? Everyone loved Pat. There, for the first time that thought snuck into her head. Everyone loved Pat. Who would be on Duffy's side? All the night questions poured over Kate. She always used to say there was a door for every Arthur, and everyone liked to be behind his own door. But they'd all come out now. It would be just like the newspaper boy's dog. She wasn't stupid. She knew. Ten days and . . . That soreness ached again, from the inside out.

"Please." J.'s face got rubbery, his eyes sad triangles. Silly kid in his slippers in the middle of the night, following her like that, shivering. What good was that stupid little cotton bathrobe, for Pete's sake. J. leaned against the fence.

Kate didn't answer him, but she stood up slowly and set Duffy down. The leash was still attached. "Just turn around," she said, stiffly. There was no need for J. to know how she had gotten inside the fence. When he turned, she pushed Duffy through the hole, crawled through herself, then brushing off her jacket started down the path with Duff behind her.

"And . . ." she shouted up without turning, "there's no need to tell anyone where I was. Not a word, J."

J. had been standing there, shivering in the shadows, when he heard her and saw her ahead of him, loping down the hill. He ran after her to catch up.

"Kate, tell me what happened. I only heard parts. Kate, what are they going to do with Duff? What's going to happen to Pat? Kate. Wait for me. Kate, wait."

THEY THOUGHT SHE WAS ASLEEP. Kate with J. curled around her feet huddled under the green blanket on the Great Brown Couch. Duff lay at Kate's head on the top cushions, his chin in her hair. A frost-mist was condensing on the large back window. It was morning gray.

"Let her sleep," Kate's mother whispered as she walked through the room toward the kitchen. "She has a lot to think about."

For once Susan was saying nothing.

"He's going to be fine, Susan. Trust the doctor."

Kate could still hear them. She knew her mother was stopping to get the teakettle. Click. The heat turned on. The scraping of a chair. Susan had sat down, facing her mother at the stove. Two cups. The instant coffee. The bread drawer and an unfolding of paper. The toaster pushed down.

Susan's voice started to crack. "He looked terrible, Mom. I couldn't tell him. But . . ."

"I know, I know, baby, but his face is swollen. That lip's not going to stay puffed up that way. And the scars . . ."

The kettle slowly gathered steam, heat sounds.

"Forty stitches, Mom. Forty." Susan's voice stretched, nearly breaking.

But there was no answer. Mother must have put her fingers to her lips. She did that often. She preferred to wait for the right moment to talk about something unpleasant. And she liked to prepare for it, wait for a quiet time. That was her way. But it didn't matter now. No one had to tell Kate. Ten days were ten days.

Kate felt that wooziness in her stomach that somehow flowed up to her mouth and head. She squinted her eyes shut. Then she heard the shuffling on the stairs, that slow shuffling. She wasn't even certain her father had talked to her mother this morning. He was sleeping when Kate sneaked back into the house. Like everyone else in the Arthur family, he more or less went his own way. Usually he didn't even speak before 11:43 on a Saturday morning. Eleven forty-three was the magic minute, he always said. It couldn't have been more than 7:30 now. The family was never in the kitchen at the same time mornings anyway, because Mother was a morning person, Susan a night person, Dad an afternoon person. Kate and J. just stayed out of everyone's way mornings.

But now Dad scuffled in. Kate expected an explosion of some kind. He usually had one a year. Something like a lion who pads around in his own world, pokes his head up through the fog, roars, then ducks down and continues exploring his own footsteps.

"Well . . ." he yawned. Not much of a roar. He almost sounded casual. "How's Pat?" No, there was something serious in his tone.

"Good. I think he'll be all right." Mother was taking out a new cup.

"Our insurance will take care of him. Anything he needs. You told the family that? They're not to worry about a thing."

Another long silence.

"Well, has anyone figured out what went wrong with the dog last night?"

The dog.

Kate looked up at the ceiling. It had been refinished using tile squares with swirls of holes. Once when she had measles she had sat on the couch and counted them out of boredom. She had forgotten the count. It seemed to her there were 464 . . . or 644. She looked up and started to count again. One. Two.

"We were on the couch . . ."

Kate remembered the blood that she had smeared on her hand when looking for Duff. It had been on the couch arm. She wondered if anyone had washed it off or whether she was lying on it now.

"Pat and I were teasing . . . well, Pat was teasing. . . ." A pause. "Do I have to go through this again?" It was Susan.

One. Two. Three. Four. Five. The dots blurred. One. Two. Three.

"Anyway," she started to speak more quietly. Someone must have shushed her. "He was trying to get me to smile. Said I looked gloomy. Grumpy. Actually, I had been thinking of breaking up with him . . . I had been. Can you imagine? It's just, he's so far away at school, and I am, too. Anyway, I just didn't know how to say it. And he was tickling me and pinching.

"And Duff came in from upstairs, pushed the door open, and tried to jump up on the couch with us. Between us."

Long pause.

"I pushed him down. 'Pushy dog,' I told him. 'It's the Ferocious Forward,' Pat shouted."

Water being poured into the cup. "Did Duff seem angry, Susan?" Kate's dad spoke as he sipped a noisy first sip.

"No. Playing. 'Down, pushy dog,' I told him. I'm always telling him to get off the furniture, you know. Never listens."

"Go on, Susan," Mother said.

Kate sucked in a huge, hurting breath. Twenty-three. Twenty-four. J. turned, heavily sprawling across her two legs, his face stretched like a rubber mask on his pillow.

"He ran around the room as if he were getting that head start he does when he tosses his bowl, then he jumped right back on the couch between us. 'Hey,' I said, 'you think you own this couch?' and I pushed him off again. I think I said something to Pat like, 'I think I need to go to bed,' but Pat got sillier, and this time tried to kiss me, but not seriously. 'I love you, my darling. You can't leave me,' or something silly like that. I tried to pull away. And suddenly . . . suddenly Duff jumped up again and . . ."

Before she could hear the last words, Kate twisted over on her face, dumping Duff from his comfortable perch and forcing J. to groan for "covers . . ." An extra pillow fell on the floor, and the kitchen voices stopped. Even the muffled sounds of cups and hands and feet stopped.

"Kate!" Mother called.

Dad's slippers shuffling across the floor. He was at the head of the couch, then he sat on the stack of magazines at her head. But Kate didn't move. No one said anything, as if waiting to see whether she were really asleep or not. Looking at her eyes. Her mouth. When she didn't move, not a hair, her mother finally whispered.

"Poor Kate. She might as well sleep. In the next ten days she has to ask some important questions . . . make some decisions . . . poor Kate."

"Well, just leave her alone." That was her father. "If anyone can handle it, Kate can."

J.'S NUMBER TWO GATLING GUNS fired across the yard. *Pah-koooooo. Pah-koooooo.* The shots, like an airy gargle, threatened the hill at the back fence.

"They're coming. I see them behind the smoke. Behind that hill!" The voice was desperate. The Rebel hat dipped behind the Gatling guns. "Damn!" a similar but huskier voice shouted. "These rocks are no good to us. It's Devil's Den all over again. We're trapped here. Trapped!" *Pah-kooooooo.* The gargle again and a "ahhhhhhhhh" painful scream.

Kate sniffled and changed the soccer ball from one hand to the other. Someone said the temperature had dropped from the sixties to the low forties during the night. She wasn't surprised. She pulled her hands up into the sleeves of her plaid lumberman's jacket. She didn't really care about the weather today.

For the first time in her fourteen years, Kate didn't know where to go.

"Watch . . . over there. Yanks! They're making a break for it!" The voice bellowed into the thunder of the cannon. *"Pah-koooooo!"*

She had tried her own bedroom first, mainly because she had this feeling that she wanted to be close to Duff. Alone. She didn't try to figure that out. She just wanted to know he was with her. So, while he nested himself into the pillow next to her, she took her newest *Soccer World* magazine out from under her mattress, the one she had been hiding from J., and started checking the ads. Until Susan's friends Sandy Nichols, Mary Levins and Roberta Whats-her-name came squealing right into her room, looking for extra magazines, saying they were going to put together this great big poster get-well card for Pat and wanted funny ads, ones that said: "He's a Smirnoff man and look what happened to him," and "Why this one-of-a-kind invention ended up as the only one of its kind." Instead of Western Electric, they would put Pat! They took over Kate's room with their Elmer's glue and their giggles. You would have thought it was a party.

Then she tried the kitchen, but that was where the phone was, and Mom had put her stack of work aside to take over the phone with a blurb that began: "He's fine, I think. His lip is swollen. He has a headache, and he's not supposed to laugh. We think he'll be all right. We're going over later. About four. I guess you should call first."

⚜ 69 ⚜

Kate's father, not able to use his potting shed because of Susan's friends coming in and out to collect the news, set up his workshop in the family room and put on Channel 13, with sound. A thousand violins. Papers all over the place. Little shovels on the Great Brown Couch.

When she and Duff found asylum on the front porch Mrs. MacGregor, the next door neighbor whom the Arthurs had seen no more than twice since the MacGregors first moved in four years ago from Alabama, met Kate to ask if the family would be so kind as to make certain Duff was never left alone in the front yard because her three-year-old sometimes put his finger through the fence.

Now Duff snuffled under the picnic table, his nose rooted in leaves, tunneling first in one pile, then shifting on his black, mechanical toy legs and snuffling out another one. Did that look like the kind of dog a person had to hide their three-year-old from? A little black Scottie who got thrilled about rousting out a field mouse and tackling flying leaves, for Pete's sake?

Maybe that was why at about three o'clock in the afternoon, with the doorbell still ringing in between phone calls and shouts for scissors, Kate got this mixed-up feeling that she wanted to be near someone. Maybe it was to say, "Look, the dog still runs after his bone, and he still sits in my hair and watches TV, and he still throws his bowls across the floor." Maybe it was to say that.

Anyway that was when Kate pulled up a chair behind her mother who sat talking on the phone to Pat's mother about some schnauzer Pat had when he was eight. A dog that had to be "put away." Kate had put her cheek on her mother's back, felt her breathing in and out, the buzz of her voice. Warm. But her mother hadn't noticed, and when Mrs. McIntyre said something funny, she had pulled away to laugh.

Of course J. was ready with a big suggestion to make pretzels, but Kate had picked up Duff and carried him into the family room, over to where her father was potting. For a long time she watched him dig up soil from a bag and carefully mix it with something that looked like sand. A little sprinkled across the floor. Kate put it back in the pot. As he reached behind her to pick up a wire pot, he brushed her hair away, then turned and bent his lanky back over his pots.

Even though everyone was there, Kate had suddenly felt alone. A new kind of alone. With no place to go.

Now she rubbed her sleeve across her nose. The backyard was as good a place as any, she guessed.

"It's a wild horse, men. Make a break while they're still distracted." J., carrying his hardy hip gun of beam of erector set and giant branch tied together with Mother's parcel string, crept out from under the porch and dashed to the dogwood trees. Kate couldn't seem to get rid of him today. So what was new.

Some kids trailed outside the back fence. It was the main pathway between Simpson's field and the street. J. didn't seem to notice them, only to say, "Hangers on. Camp bums." He gritted his teeth and burst out again to the mulch pile. "Perfect cover," he muttered. Relieved.

Duff, who had sped behind J. to the mulch pile, nosed his black snout along the leaf-packed edge, then catching an interesting smell, dashed a few more feet along it and nosed again.

"Duff's got a mouse!" J. announced temporarily out of uniform. Quickly, he checked both sides to see if anyone had heard him, and dropped to his belly, looking for the next cover: an old kitchen door, which had one time been on its way to the town dump, now pitched against the back fence.

Kate dropped her soccer ball near the table and jumped down next to it. Then, she dribbled it through the leaves, first right, left, left, then to the right. Around a stump of a tree that had never been cut down but was still full of a woodpecker's family, around an overturned wheelbarrow.

Duff cut the ball off just past the wheelbarrow.

"Thief!" Kate called.

J. darted to the overturned door, leaped under it, and

rolled over. "Ahhhhhhhhhhhh," he wailed a dramatic death.

Kate spun around the tree and stole the ball from Duff, who barked competitively at her heels, then ran ahead to the ball, yelping all the way.

Neither of them saw the three girls at the fence.

"Hey, Kate." Of all people, it was Kathy Ryan dressed in white soccer shorts with a blue stripe around the round edges and a blue T-shirt with a felt jacket over her shoulders. Her round face looked rounder for the short curls she had since her last hair-cut and perm. Her freckles ran together, almost as bad as J.'s. Freckles even on her neck and arms.

"Hey," Kate answered. She blushed for some dumb reason. Maybe because she wondered if Kathy saw her playing soccer with Duff and the trees. Duff stood with the ball under his chin, as if he had no intention of stopping the game. After all a game was a game.

"I heard about Pat."

Great, that was all Kate needed.

"Is that the dog there?" the other girl asked. A Nancy something. Kate didn't really know what. One of the girls who had come to Central from the other junior high. Kate never liked her even from afar.

"Look at the teeth on that dog. Fangs." She had a hoarse voice.

Kate picked up her soccer ball and bit the inside of

her cheek. The backyard hadn't been such a great place to come after all. J. stopped shelling the nest of Yankees by the garage.

The girl, who was not wearing soccer clothes, had long blond hair that made her narrow face look even narrower. Half-wide blue eyes gave her a look of mischief. But not like Pat's. She turned and looked around.

"Have you seen Pat yet?" Kathy seemed to ignore her.

Kate turned suddenly and looked back up at the door. Duff really had had enough time outside anyway. And now that she thought about it, she hated nosy people.

"Pat McIntyre. Isn't that who Duff bit, Kate?"

She nodded. Boy, this was one of the craziest things. A person couldn't find a place to be around her own house. Crazy.

"He's such a nice kid," the quieter Marie said. "Fifty stitches in the mouth, I heard."

They were not only gossipy, but wrong.

The blond girl stooped down by the fence and pushed a good sized stick through. "Here, Tiger," she teased.

"Stop it," Kathy said, then turned to Kate. "Anyway, if you see Pat, tell him we hope he gets better quick."

The girl waggled the stick. "Tiger, hey, monster, come here. Bite my stick with those fangs!" Duff pricked his ears at the rustling in the leaves.

"Hey," Kate said. "Leave him alone."

"Look, Kathy, he's coming. Here, monster. Here, monster." She laughed gleefully as Duff sped through the leaves like a water-skier plowing up waves. But when he got within ten feet or so, he stopped and started to growl. Kate tried to listen to which growl it was. She felt that wooziness swell up in her stomach. The girl's hand wiggled all the way through the fence.

Duff growled again.

"This is great! Look, Kathy, he's really crazy! Afraid of a stick? Or me?" She laughed and sat down on the ground by the fence.

Kate didn't even look at Kathy. "Just take your hand out of my yard," she said. She guessed saying "my" yard was two-year-old stuff, but how else did you talk to someone that stupid.

The girl finally looked up. "All right. Nasty, aren't we?" She rattled the stick one more time and stood up.

"Kate!" Susan shouted from the family room door.

"Listen, Kate," Kathy said. "I'm sorry it had to be Duff. I always liked that silly mutt. I still remember the day he wouldn't let us out the front door when we wanted to go to the movies . . . sprawled. . . ."

"Like a starched shirt."

The girl, Nancy, glared at Duff. Duff glared back.

"Kate!" Susan called again.

Kathy went on, "Well, anyway, Kate. Stop by some time and play with us. You'd like the girls from East. Paul's coaching."

Paul.

"Kate, I'm only going to call you one more time!"

"I'll see you, Kate." Kathy waved again. Her blue eyes looked a little sad. "Bye, Duff," she said. Nancy stood with her jaw out. "Oh, come on, Nancy. Leave them alone."

The three girls had already turned their backs and were walking down the path that cut through the woods before it reached the open field. Nancy was laughing and shaking the stick as if she were acting out the little drama again. Kathy threw the soccer ball to Marie. Their feet shuffled through the piles of leaves.

"Hey, Kate, want to play Stratego? I've hid a new soccer magazine in my Lego box, want to read the ads? Want to make up our own story for the three o'clock *Little Rascals?*" J. added questions, like someone adding on a calculator as Kate walked up the stairs and into the family room.

But before she could scream "Quiet!" at him, Susan met her.

"Are you deaf, Kate?" She carried a box full of newspaper-wrapped articles of all shapes. "We're going to see Pat. Would you like to come?"

Kate walked over to the couch and sat down. Duff helicoptered himself up beside her and burrowed into the green blanket.

"I'm not going to beg you. Do you want to come or not?"

That stomach again, for Pete's sake.

"I'd go with you, Kate." J. said. "I have some of my soup left. Pat would like that soup. I like Pat."

Dumb kid.

Susan stared. "Well, I guess that means no. I'm not surprised. What could be more entertaining than sitting all day on the couch with that dog. Would you like me to put the television on?"

That was when Kate knew where she wanted to go.

"THAT IS ABSOLUTELY RIDICULOUS." Mr. Arthur pushed his glasses up on his nose. His hands had a layer of soot, his fingernails were black. "She was just here. On the couch."

Mrs. Arthur called up the stairs. "Kate?" She turned back toward the family room. "Charles, did you look in the backyard?"

"She's not in the backyard," J. muttered. He sat between two strings which ran from the TV set to his Lego fort across the room, but his airplanes were sitting still at the top.

"That's ridiculous. It's nearly dark, it looks like rain—heavy clouds. She wouldn't be in the backyard." Mr. Arthur closed his eyes with finality.

"Well then, where is she? Is Duffy gone, too?" Mrs. Arthur pushed her graying hair back and walked quickly into the kitchen and pulled the chairs out so that she could see under the table. When Kate was little, she used to spend vast amounts of time under the table playing with her knives and forks. The knives were the good guys. She wasn't there. Neither was Duff.

Mr. Arthur sat back, meditating against the glass door. "I remember she was sitting next to me for a while when I was transferring soil from the clay pot to the wire pot. I couldn't get that soil balance right, Mae. I swear, there is something acidic about the air here."

"And she was with me at the telephone for a while, before I dropped over to see Pat," Mrs. Arthur said.

J. twisted his lips in disgust. "She was on the couch a long time after that."

"She's pouting somewhere," Susan said, coming into the room. She let herself drop onto the couch. "Probably in some closet. Imagine a fourteen-year-old pouting in a closet! I mean, you'd think *we* did something wrong." Her eyes looked tired.

Mrs. Arthur brushed Susan's hair back. "You only got two hours of sleep last night, chicken," she said. Then with her hands on her hips, she stood up. "Look how dark it is. Maybe she's in the attic." That was another Kate hideout in years past; she spent a lot of time up there in the sixth grade when she formed that club of three with Kathy Ryan and Buzz Taylor, the boy who moved away.

Mrs. Arthur took the stairs by twos, which was no easy thing for her. Then she pulled the rope ladder down and climbed up the springy attic stairway. White mounds cluttered the boards.

"She's not here!" Mrs. Arthur called down.

"I could have told her that," J. mumbled. He took one of his airplanes and winged it down the string. It narrowly missed Mr. Arthur sitting on his papers like a yogi.

Susan leaned forward, slowly stood up, and pulled the phone over on her lap. She dialed, thought a moment, and dialed again. And waited. "Is Kathy there?" Pause. "Kathy? Susan Arthur. Have you seen Kate? Yes. I remember. Not since then . . . all right. If you do, Kathy, call us. Oh, I'm sure. Just a walk." Susan shrugged, hung up, then went toward the basement door. "Downstairs anyone?" she called back.

"Hmmmmmmmmm," Mr. Arthur looked at his fingers. "That's probably what she did. Went for a walk."

J. sent another plane. "I doubt it," he said to himself.

Finally, Mr. Arthur put his pot down and wiped his hands off on a towel. "J. You're saying no to everything, old sport. I am beginning to have the distinct feeling you know something you're not sharing. Do you know where Kate is?"

J. shrugged, bit his lips together, and picked up another plane and winged it.

His father sat down in front of him and tapped his

lips. "Do you think she went for a walk?"

J. shrugged a tentative: sort of.

"Ah . . . the plot thickens . . . did she walk *some-where?*"

"I don't see her down here," Susan yelled up through the stairwell. "I'll look in the garage."

J. stuck out his chin in a positive maybe.

Mr. Arthur clicked his tongue. ". . . and was the somewhere across the ravine . . ."

J. dropped his eyes. Negative.

"Simpson's field?"

An impatient sigh. Mr. Arthur recrossed his legs and thought into his hands. "Or . . ." he suddenly burst out, "down the street toward Tower Hill?"

J.'s eyes widened and he bit his mouth harder.

"J., can't you just tell me? I feel as if I were playing 'red hot'—'ice cold.' "

J. turned his back and went back to his planes.

"All right, all right. Let me see . . . would she be . . . up *on* the hill?"

J. turned around and blinked possibility at his father, just as Mrs. Arthur came in dusting a stringy cobweb off her arm. "Honestly, Charles, I don't know where those two are. I just don't know."

Mr. Arthur got up and stamped his feet on the fireplace hearth, shaking the black dust from his pants, then he squeezed Mrs. Arthur's shoulder. "I'll be back," he said. "Don't worry."

J. winged a last plane, pleased. He hadn't said a word.

KATE THOUGHT SHE HAD BROUGHT her scarf, too, but at least this time she had her hat. It was brown and cream colored and stretchy, and she pulled it down nearly to her chin. The knapsack that sat next to her was lumpy with her afghan, bologna and sprout sandwich and four year-old *Soccer World* magazines. She had forgotten how quickly it got dark at this time of year. She could have brought her flashlight, too. It was too big and red, but waterproof. Kate settled into the weed-covered pothole the way Duff did into her pillow or couch cushion. It still wasn't soft.

The water tower's light had been flickering its red warning light as she mounted the path. But there was no light under here. Only the giant friendly legs. A funny thought that they might walk on down the hill and across the ravine and Simpson's field struck her.

"Escaped water tower," the headlines would read. "Footprints heading west." She looked up at the water-filled belly.

Duff was scuffling with some particularly ornery weed-covered burrows by the metal fence. He yelped one quick spike of a yelp, then burrowed into the denlike covering so that only his wagging bottom and SOS tail stuck out. Then, in a spin, he ran all the way back to Kate, shoved his front paws against her knees, and ran away again.

"Telling your mama, huh, you big baby." Kate smiled. Every time she played with Duff today, she felt a thick something in her chest. But she really hadn't put any words to it. It was just something that sat there like an undigested piece of peanut butter. At least she didn't feel as alone here as she had at home. And there was no hurry. No one would miss them for a while. That was for sure. The lump seemed to feel bigger. And she could count on J. to keep his mouth shut. At least he was good for that. Silly little twerp with his Confederate war waging seven days a week.

Kate sketched out a circle in the dirt, drew spindles in it, then she started to walk the circle, when she heard something rattle the fence behind her. It sent a shiver through her and she quietly sank behind a leg. She didn't even try to see what caused the rattling. She didn't move. But Duff started to bark at it, whatever it was.

"Kate!" It was her father. Still she didn't move.

"Kate . . . babe?" When she didn't answer, he walked around the edges of the fence, slowly, trying to look inside the fence, darker tonight than last night because of the clouds. He felt his way with one hand. Even without looking directly at him, Kate could see he still had on his white potting coat under his jacket. He looked like an escaped mad scientist. Duff sprang to the fence, stood for a moment like a statue, sniffed at the feet, then started to wag his whole second part.

"Hi, Duff," Kate's father said. He looked through one of the diamond links at Kate hunched up against the leg of the water tower. "Hi, Katie," he said. She always remembered his soft voice, a voice she always figured would sound wonderful singing "Greensleeves," her favorite folk song. With a guitar background.

"Come sit by me, Kate," Mr. Arthur called as he settled down outside the fence. Kate had to smile at his red-tassled ski hat. He really didn't ski anymore, but he wore that hat everywhere, to the drugstore, on the train to the city with all those stodgy businessmen, even to dinner sometimes. "Come on, Babe."

Kate wanted to—she could feel that somewhere around the peanut butter lump. But she couldn't. Duffy backed into another burrow and scuffled.

"You know, Kate. This is quite a place you've got here. A little chilly, but private. Accommodations look good. Unless it rains, of course." He grinned at her. "Or snows . . ." Kate looked down at her hands wound inside each other inside her jacket sleeves.

"And that's quite a lamp you have there," he said, looking up at the tower.

"A mushroom," Kate said, still looking at her hands.

"Well," Mr. Arthur leaned his shoulder against the fence. "I bet it's the kind that walks away in the night."

Kate couldn't believe he had said that.

"Yep, right down the hill. Can you imagine its footprints!"

The red light on top of the tower cast an eerie rose glow across the field and huddled bushes. Kate wondered why she couldn't get up and walk over to the fence. That wouldn't hurt. But she couldn't move.

"You know, Kate, I had a dog once." Mr. Arthur had to talk pretty loud to carry across the fenced-in field. "Did I ever tell you?" He never had. A long time ago he used to read her stories of Winnie-the-Pooh under the covers with a flashlight. To get into the mood, he always said. But he never told her about a dog. "His name was Buster, of all things. A corny name. He wasn't soft, Kate, like some dogs. He was some mix of retriever and terrier, one ear up and one mangled from some scrap he had before he wandered half-dead onto our porch. Boy, was he scrappy. And muscley. And big. We'd have these wrestling matches every morning."

Something in the trees nearby rustled and Mr. Arthur and Kate waited, but whatever it was didn't move again.

"He'd walk me to school. Dumb dog. And one day," Mr. Arthur started to laugh. He often did this. Something would tickle him and he'd laugh and laugh before anyone knew why.

Yes? Kate wanted to say.

"He waited in the bushes by the school after I went in . . ." He laughed, "and when someone opened the door, zap, in he snuck between legs, and ran down the high school hall." He laughed again, wiping his eyes underneath his glasses and shaking his head. It was like the gingerbread man. The chemistry teacher tried to catch him. Old Mr. Tender, the janitor, tried to catch him. Mrs. Sorenson, the busty principal, waddled after him. I finally saw them running all in a line, but he outran them, every one, and ran straight to me, in history. This big tear-eared old mutt."

Mr. Arthur chuckled like a motor that had been shut off but had to wind down. "Big tear-eared old mutt," he said again. "He outlived a knock by a United Parcel truck, poisoning by crochety old Mrs. Simpson, getting scratched by Jenny, a big yellow neighborhood cat. Finally dumb old dog, he got blind and deaf . . .

"That scared him some." His laughing had run out. "And he started growling at kids."

Kate suddenly turned around to see where her black shadow had run himself now. When he brushed up against her, she pulled him onto her lap and rubbed her cheek against his big clown head.

"One day he nipped at a neighbor kid. Scared the kid all the way home. I don't think he would have done anything, but my dad whopped him good . . . and. . . ." Mr. Arthur looked through the triangle again.

"Come here, Kate. You know I'm not good at shouting. How'll I be able to sing 'Faustus' in the shower?"

Kate took a long look at her knapsack, then she hiked Duff into her arms and walked slowly over to the fence and sat down cross-legged. She wasn't giving in or anything, just because she had walked a few feet. Just listening. What was wrong with that.

"I can still feel that scruffy yellow hair. And those gray whiskers all over his nose. Silly mutt."

There was this funny silence and the rosy light blinking silently on and off, on and off. Mr. Arthur stared into the trees. Funny, Kate had never thought of her father as a dog person; he was always more of a plant and art and opera person. But that was dumb. How many kids were plant and art and opera people when they were fifteen years old.

Mr. Arthur started up again. "Well, when he couldn't see and he couldn't hear and he didn't know that he couldn't go scaring three-year-olds, I knew I had to decide what to do with him. Maybe I was sixteen then."

Duff bounded off on another tour of the yard, then came up behind Kate and leaned against her back as if she were a lamppost. He felt warm there, and Kate could feel his deep breathing from his sprint. And she realized there were tears in her again.

Mr. Arthur put his fingers against the fence, but the triangles were too small for him to reach through. "It took a lot of thinking, Kate. A lot. I still feel it, like a hole in my chest." A little like a spoonful of peanut butter stuck there. Yes, she knew that feeling.

"Sometimes, there's no way to get away from something. No way."

Kate shook her head. As the moon moved out between grumbling gray clouds on the horizon, the water tower legs stretched darker down the hill behind her father. Not running yet.

THE SHADOW THAT KATE SAW rising up behind her father was thin and willowy.

"Dad?" it called, not too sure of itself. Susan. Kate knew that Susan was as thrilled about the dark as she was. There had been times when they were little when the two of them would not go downstairs at night without each other. Hand in hand, they would tackle one step at a time, wait, then try another. They figured that each of them would protect the other. A four-year-old and a nine-year-old, for Pete's sake. Kate nearly smiled.

"Dad?" Susan called out tentatively again.

When she saw his cross-legged yogi self by the fence, she strode faster up the hill. Then she caught sight of Kate on the other side of the fence. Kate felt her insides get tight, and she was ready for Susan's scream.

"Kate?" That soft?

"Oh, hello honey," her dad said as if he had just

accidentally run into her at the local drugstore. "We're just talking."

Susan tucked her skirt under her, crouched down next to her father and looked up at the water tower. "Ah, I thought you were having a picnic."

Kate's father squeezed Susan's shoulder. "No. Just talking. About dumb dogs."

Kate still felt Duff warm against her back.

"Dogs! What about hamsters? Remember Othello, Kate?"

Mr. Arthur screwed his forehead into a painful recollection. "That's not the one who got its leg broken turning his exercise wheel so hard in the middle of the night?"

Susan looked over at Kate and grinned.

Mr. Arthur continued. "The one whose leg the veterinarian fixed with a popsicle stick?"

Susan nodded.

"Painful memory, Susan. Imagine my bill: 25 cents for popsicle stick."

Kate smiled inside her jacket collar, but as the other two huddled together, a third shadow rustled up the path into the flickering tower light. It was Mrs. Arthur.

"Charles? . . . Susan? Oh, Kate." Mrs. Arthur could bicycle ten miles a day, but climbing anything with more than a two-degree angle winded her. She even avoided ladders. Now she put her hands on her hips, glanced briefly at Kate again, and puffed.

"I never was one for nighttime picnics. Come on, gang, let's go."

"Now, now, Mae. This isn't a picnic, it's a meeting, and I called it!"

A small shadow hovered at the edge of the path.

"Come on, J., you too," Mr. Arthur said. The shadow didn't move. Without seeing his eyes Kate knew J. was watching her. He knew she hated finks. "A good thing I found Kate's scarf on the trail, J. You sure weren't helping me. I never would have found your sister. Probably a conspiracy."

The shadow side-stepped slowly toward Mrs. Arthur, but Susan took his leg, and as he crouched down, she unzipped her coat, pulled him onto her lap and folded him inside her jacket. "Squirt," she said, nestling her chin in his hair.

"Now, the subject of the meeting is . . . animal stories we have known and survived," Mr. Arthur said in his Monday-morning accountant voice.

"You know, like the story of the seagull with the broken wing . . ." Susan said.

". . . or the rabbit who got caught in the milk box?" J. whispered.

"I get it," Mrs. Arthur started, "you mean, like the story of the man who thought a baby robin was a hawk."

"Oh, that story's not worth mentioning . . ." Mr. Arthur tipped his ski-capped head back and looked up at the sky.

". . . and," Mrs. Arthur went on anyway, "fed it ground beef steak twenty-four hours a day . . ."

". . . now Mae . . ."

". . . and took it for walks . . ."

"This is ridiculous."

"And let it sleep on the end of his bed."

Susan started to smile into J.'s hair.

"It might have been a valuable hawk . . . or even an eagle." Mr. Arthur looked mystical.

"It had a red breast, Charles."

J. looked up at Susan and caught her wink. Kate dug her nose deeper into her collar to swallow a laugh, and Mrs. Arthur glanced sideways from one to the other of them, then tilted her head at Mr. Arthur, who finally returned a grudging smile.

Then, for a strange moment none of them said anything. Or even moved. It was as if there were a string between them. Not a string you see, like J.'s rope webs that he set up for his planes and you tripped on. This was a string that connected. Kate slowly scratched Duff's neck, which he stretched up like a goose swallowing water. She was afraid to move too much for fear she'd break the string.

Finally, Mrs. Arthur huddled deeper into her coat. "Well," she said. Kate just knew she was going to be practical.

"Well," Mr. Arthur said, reaching into his side pocket. He just couldn't be practical, too. "Maybe a picnic's not a bad idea after all." He pulled out a half stick of gum and an opened Snickers bar. "How's this?" he said.

Kate glanced quickly at Mrs. Arthur, but she wasn't getting up. She had her hands in the side pockets of her woolly coat and was pulling out a wrapped pack of crackers.

"Hmmmmmmm," Mr. Arthur murmured approvingly, then turned toward Susan. She had caught on, too. Already she had reached into her pocket and pulled out what looked like a Certs wrapper and some raisins.

Even J. struggled to get into his jeans pockets and finally pulled out a handful of lint-covered jelly beans, peanuts and a chewed piece of bubble gum, which he proudly delivered into his father's hands.

They all seemed to avoid looking at Kate, but they needn't have. She had suddenly stood up, and without saying anything, run over to the knapsack and pulled out a package. As she walked back she unfolded the hastily wrapped plastic and tore off a small part of the bulging sandwich. The rest she fed through the fence.

"Mmmmmmmmmmm," Mr. Arthur murmured as he

divided the gum, nuts, jelly beans, raisins, sandwich and Snickers bar into equal parts. Then they all ate. Quietly. Kate let Duff lick the crackers off her hands and popped her piece of the sandwich into her mouth, tucking some stray sprouts in at the last second. Too bad she had forgotten mustard. Susan and her father liked mustard.

When he was finished, Mr. Arthur sat back and dabbed his mouth with his neatly squared handkerchief. "Mmmmmmm," he murmured again.

Behind them, across the field, the moon looked like a balloon someone had let go. It floated free, up into the sky, above the clouds. There was a gray ring around it, and the trees looked like chilly silhouettes as a brisk cold wind rattled branches. Kate hated to admit it, but hat or no hat, she was cold to the bone. The only warm spot on her whole body was where Duff had nested against her legs. Even her big toe felt numb inside her shoe, but she wasn't going to be the one who suggested going home.

It was a long time before Mr. Arthur finally said, "As much as I like nighttime meetings . . . and picnics, it's time to go home." He looked at Kate, but he said, "You too, Duff."

Kate got up creakily, and as the others walked toward the path and waited, Mr. Arthur walked along the fence with Kate toward the hole beneath the gate.

She threw her knapsack under first, then she slipped the leash on Duff and handed it through to her father who pulled him slowly under the gate. Kate crawled after him.

The path really felt like a tunnel now with the bushes bowing stiffly overhead. The others walked well ahead. Her father scratched Kate's back as they picked their way through the tunnel.

"You do know, Kate, there is more than one possibility for Duff," her father started.

"For ten days," Kate said sarcastically. "Then . . . automatically . . ."

"No. Wrong. Not automatically anything. Is that what you thought, Katie? After all, Duff's not bitten a raft of people."

He seemed to be saying there was more than one possibility.

"Katie, that's one of the reasons we need the ten days. To think."

Kate watched her dad's face. He seemed to be telling the truth. "Duff did believe he was protecting Susan, Dad, I'm sure of that."

"Me, too, Kate."

"And it's only been a few days since he was at the vet's . . ."

"True, Kate."

"And he really is the same dog . . . you saw him."

"It seems that way."

Ahead of them the street lamps flickered in a settling mist. As they passed the brown bungalow, Kate looked up. Kathy's bedroom light was still on.

"We just need time, Kate. You need time." He paused, "You might even want to go see your old buddy, Pat, while you're thinking."

Kate found herself biting the inside of her cheek again. "Dad," she finally said. "What happened to Buster?"

"Well . . . before I had a chance to make a decision, Buster snuck out the screen door one day. Blind and deaf, he chased a bread truck. The driver never saw him. You see, Kate, sometimes decisions are taken away from us, too."

THE BEST THING ABOUT THAT NIGHT was that Kate felt sleepy. Mrs. Arthur brought her a cup of hot chocolate and a stack of Oreo cookies, then she got Grandma's old feather quilt out of the cedar chest and piled that on top of Kate's blanket. Susan insisted on putting on a stack of her Beatles records for Kate. Duffy curled himself around her hair. Kate had to admit it, she felt warm, finally. Feathery, hot chocolate warm and sleepy.

Even the ideas that seemed to crowd in her head, most of them, seemed clearer.. It made sense that people could feel bad for Duff and feel bad for Pat, too. Was she dumb not to see that. Even ten-year-old geniuses could have figured that one out. It just followed that she'd go to see Pat tomorrow. Maybe she'd take him that *Soccer World* magazine. Lord, she hoped his lip was going to be all right. He was too gorgeous not to stay that way. Running down the field or tackling J. behind the plants. Maybe she'd let J.

bring some of his dumb Confederate soup. It would turn green and fuzzy in the refrigerator if someone didn't eat it.

And she began to see another double. That Duffy could be a problem, but didn't have to be put to sleep. There were signs like: Beware, Dog Bites. People just had to be warned. Duff had only bitten once. With reason. He didn't go around biting everyone, the mailman, the package man, three-year-old kids, for Pete's sake.

"You are a silly, old clown," Kate kept saying to Duff, but before she had even finished her hot chocolate, Duff was dead weight, snoring into her hair. All those field mice up by the tower. But that was all Kate remembered, because it was so warm, and she was so tired.

Maybe that was why she was surprised next morning when she woke up with a cold. Her eyes watery. Her nose stuffed. The water tower might have been a wonderful place to visit, but it was miserably chilly in October at night. Kate had the slightest recollection that her parents had poked their heads in to say they were going to buy peat moss and J. wanted to go along, and that Susan was going to go over to read to Pat. None of it concerned Kate. She kept waking up, noticing how stuffed she felt, that the house was empty, and dozing off again.

How many times she had wakened and drifted back to sleep Kate wasn't sure. And how many times the front doorbell rang, she wasn't sure. When she finally heard it, she thought it was part of a dream she had been having about a ravine next to a dried-up stream where there were these giant footprints.

But then, she felt Duff drop down off her bed, and when she turned over, she saw his tail disappear out the cracked door.

The "Yooooooohooooooo" downstairs surprised her. Someone had just walked into the house.

"Mae!" a voice called. "Mae!" It sounded like Mrs. Jackson. Someone else would get it. Kate burrowed in her pillow. Her head felt as if it were stuffed with wet cotton. But then she remembered no one else was home, and she heard the voice again.

"I've brought your vacuum cleaner back! Mae . . . your . . ." but she broke her sentence off midway. Faintly, Kate could hear a familiar sound. A low growl.

She sprang out of her bed with no slippers, no bathrobe, and ran down the hall and down the stairs.

In the front hall Mrs. Jackson stood holding a silvery machine with a red and black puffy bag draped on it. She was staring at McDuff.

"It's me, honey," she went on cheerily.

Kate stopped on the landing. "Mrs. Jackson," she said quietly. "You must get away from the vacuum cleaner." She said it more and more slowly, drawing out her words. At the same time she moved down the last stairs.

Duff's lips snarled around his teeth. He inched toward the machine, toward the metally mouth that seemed to snarl at him.

"But, honey old dog," Mrs. Jackson went on in her Oklahoma accent, "I love dogs. Dogs know that. Come here, old Duff," she said, walking slowly toward him. "Dogs aren't dumb, Kate. They know who is friendly toward them, that's for certain. I'm not afraid, Kate."

No time. "Don't move, Mrs. Jack . . ." But Mrs. Jackson had bent over, her hand thrust out, and before Kate could get the words out, Duff leaped and his sharp teeth folded around the outstretched hand.

KATE DIDN'T HEAR THE KNOB TWIST, the door open, and the whispers. She didn't hear J. ask what had happened and why was Kate sitting in the middle of the kitchen floor with Duff and what was going to happen now? Kate didn't see her father watch her from the kitchen door, nor her mother put her hand on her father's shoulder. She didn't even see Susan go into the dining room and sit on a chair all alone mumbling, "Oh, God."

Kate sat in the middle of the kitchen floor holding Duffy, his clown head resting on her shoulder, his feet at first struggling against her squeeze, then settling back on her shoulder. His heart pounded. He had saved them all again. From the shiny silver monsters. From the people who wanted to hurt them. That must be why Kate was scratching the back of his neck. He stretched his neck up to feel the best of it.

Kate couldn't look at his moon eyes. She could just feel his scratchy fur rubbing against her cheek. And it occurred to her suddenly that she hadn't brushed him since he had come home from the vet. And that she hadn't fed him yet this morning. And that thought put the hole back in her stomach. For some reason, those thoughts did it. Then she stopped thinking. She just sat there with him in the middle of the kitchen floor, not seeing or hearing or thinking anything.

Her father sat down next to her. "Dad," she said, and turned to her mother, too. "Mom. Is the vet's open on Sunday?"

What had happened had taken the decision out of her hands.

NOT ONLY DID THE GREAT BROWN couch stand empty in the middle of the family room, but the piles of magazines were gone, the string which ran the length of the room had disappeared, and all of the potting papers had been tucked into the fireplace for the next fire. Kate leaned against the couch.

Everyone else was in bed. It was over. She looked out the window where winter frost gathered in crystals on the screen which hadn't been taken down. The trees looked spindly out there, like stringy phantoms. She could still feel Duffy in her arms, his sturdy little sergeant self. He never did cuddle into her arms like Kathy's cocker spaniel. He was always ready for the next pounce, the next burrow, the next flying piece of hide. Those ridiculous moon eyes and fuzzy eyebrows. Kate had hung on so tight.

She grabbed a pillow off the couch and lay back on it across the middle of the floor. One bite was a mistake. A fluke. Caused by a scare at the veterinarian's. A feeding person rattling his cage and making him think people were trying to hurt him. Trying to protect his people. One bite. Something you didn't do again. But two bites . . .

"It's not our Duff," Mr. Arthur had said later. "Something's happened inside Duff's head. A terrible scare. Who knows. But he's not himself, Kate."

Kate had thought of that when she tried to stop Mrs. Jackson. Just like she had thought that probably a punctured hand would heal. But it could be the three-year-old through the fence next time. Or one of J.'s friends coming in when she wasn't there. Or someone carrying a package, something that looked rattly. Or someone punching her or someone else in the family playfully. Or . . . anything. Like his mama, Duff was a watchdog.

Kate had ridden in the car with him. She wasn't going to let him go alone. Seeing the vet's sign out front was the part she remembered. That awful black-and-white sign. Still remembered.

"Kate?" That freckled, wide-eyed voice called in the family room door. "I want to sit with you."

Kate nodded. She didn't even move away when J. leaned up against her arm. For a long time neither of them said anything.

Then finally Kate said, "You know, J., right now, while we're sitting here in the middle of the floor, it seems as if we're the center of the world, the center of the universe, with everyone and everything spinning around us. That lunchroom lady. The water tower. Even the Washington Monument." They had visited it a year ago, climbed all those steps.

J. rubbed his back against her arm. It was Mary Poppins again. Spinning and speeding.

"But, J., listen to this. Did you ever think that right now, while we're sitting here, an old man in Russia is eating his breakfast in front of a fire? He doesn't even know we exist, J."

J. looked at her, properly amazed.

"And, J., in some mysterious cloudy mountain community in Tibet, that's near China, thirty-five or fifty priests are digging a garden. With long robes on."

That was hard to believe.

"Yes, J., and in Australia, aborigines, they're like Indians, are out roping horses right now. Things are going on all over the place. You know, J., we're *not* the center of the world. Isn't that something?"

Poof, went Mary Poppins. The molten mass seemed more under control. J. breathed out a huge relieved sigh and Kate grinned at him. He was something else.

The wintery trees eased their shadows across the room. How funny the room looked, clean except for the shadows and the year-old Christmas wreath. Kate started to scratch J.'s back, and his shoulders sank and rolled comfortably as she hit the itchy spots. Kate smiled. J. did know what quiet meant. Tomorrow wouldn't be the same. Something was missing. Some-one. But maybe they'd go for a walk up past the soccer field. Just for a look.

PATRICIA LEE GAUCH grew up in Michigan and attended Miami University in Ohio. After college she wrote for newspapers for several years and then turned to writing children's books. Her picture books include *Once Upon a Dinkelsbühl, On To Widecombe Fair,* and *The Little Friar Who Flew.* She has also written the well-read *This Time, Tempe Wick?* and *The Impossible Major Rogers.*

Ms. Gauch has written two other novels, *The Green of Me* and *Fridays,* for which she has been praised by *The New York Times* as being, "A gifted writer who has something to say in her own voice, and on her own terms."

Presently, Ms. Gauch lives with her husband and three children in northern New Jersey where, in addition to writing, she teaches a children's literature course at Rutgers University.